A Piggy Pickle

HAVE YOU READ

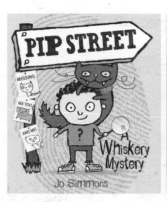
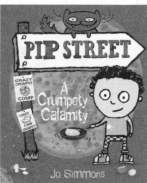

PIP STREET

A Piggy Pickle

Jo Simmons

Illustrated by Steve Wells

SCHOLASTIC

First published in the UK in 2014 by Scholastic Children's Books
An imprint of Scholastic Ltd
Euston House, 24 Eversholt Street
London, NW1 1DB, UK
Registered office: Westfield Road, Southam, Warwickshire, CV47 0RA
SCHOLASTIC and associated logos are trademarks and/or registered trademarks of
Scholastic Inc.

ISBN 978 1 407 13283 9

A CIP catalogue record for this book is available
from the British Library.

Printed and bound by CPI Group (UK) Ltd, Croydon, CR0 4YY
Papers used by Scholastic Children's Books are made from
wood grown in sustainable forests.

1 3 5 7 9 10 8 6 4 2

This is a work of fiction. Names, characters, places, incidents
and dialogues are products of the author's imagination or are used fictitiously.
Any resemblance to actual people, living or dead, events
or locales is entirely coincidental.

www.scholastic.co.uk/zone
www.visitpipstreet.com

For my resident Mr Bean-alike

1
The Black!

Pip Street. Winter. The days are short. The nights are long. The weather is rubbish. There is zero outdoor fun to be had so, instead, Bobby Cobbler is reading in his bedroom.

Bobby lives at number 4 Pip Street. If you haven't met him before, here are some things Bobby likes: being nine, living on Pip Street and having tiny Imelda Small,

1

who lives next door, for a best friend. And there's more... Bobby likes Richard Keiths, his oldie neighbour who drives a speedy mobility scooter. He likes his cat Conkers, and he likes drawing, thinking and reading (sometimes all at the same time).

Now, on this gloomy afternoon, Bobby is reading his new library book *Folklore's Freaky Creatures*. The animal that has caught Bobby's eye is a weird, ancient beast called a spookhog.

2

"A spookhog is a small, evil pig with hypnotic powers, which delights in turning men mad and spreading mischief," Bobby read. "One has not been seen in this country since Sir Thomas Twiddlefudge recorded a spookhogging incident in Donny on the Wold, Lincolnshire, in 1876. Some experts believe there are spookhogs still alive today, but there is little evidence to support this."

Carrot cake crumbs, thought Bobby, studying the page. *I wouldn't want to meet one of those on a dark—*

But before he could finish his thought, the lights went out.

Bobby sat still. Frozen. He didn't dare move.

His heart drummed in his chest. His breathing was fast. His palms were clammy.

"What's happened?" he asked, his voice a teeny bit high and squeaky.

I'll tell you. It was a blackout. A sudden, strange power cut. The whole of Pip Street had no electricity and every single light was O-U-T: OUT! It was dark. More than just dark, actually. *Really* dark. Darker than dark chocolate.

In the houses, people were groping about for candles, matches, torches. All Bobby's neighbours – the Rhubarbs, the Pasty family, Richard Keiths – were searching for a light.

But not Bobby. He could hardly think, let alone move. He stared around his dark room, trying to see something – anything. But all he could see was nothing. Nothing as far as the eye could see, if you see what I mean. His faithful cat, Conkers, was somewhere nearby, but Conkers was black and the room was black – what chance did Bobby have of finding him? Forget about it!

5

"What's happened?" he said again, nervously.

What *had* happened? Not just to the lights, but to brave, smart Bobby who loves thinking up plans and solving mysteries. The truth is,  Bobby was afraid. No, scared. No, more than that – he was *terrified* of the dark! It made him tremble, like a tiny shivering Chihuahua tied up outside a newsagent's. The dark just scared the cockles out of him, plain and simple. But then, Bobby is only human and we humans are all scared of something, aren't we? Even if it's just hair washes or Marmite.

6

After what seemed like hours, Bobby finally noticed a weak light creeping towards his room. He held his breath as the glow grew stronger. Then a bright beam dazzled his eyes.

"Only me, love," said Mrs Cobbler, shining a torch on him. "What a nuisance, eh? A power cut!"

They hugged.

"Ooh, you're trembling," she said. "Poor you. You really hate the dark, don't you?'"

Bobby nodded.

"Never mind," said his mother, "I'm sure this will be over soon and you'll never have to worry about power cuts again."

2
Where Has All the Power Gone?

How wrong could Mrs Cobbler be? Really wrong – that's how wrong. This was no one-off power cut. This was the beginning of a *plague* of power cuts that would strike Pip Street night after night.

At first, no one understood what was going on.

A bit after that, maybe a day or so later, still no one understood what was going on.

8

Then, suddenly! No one understood what was going on.

What *was* going on?

It was a good question, and one that Mrs Rhubarb had just asked Mrs Cobbler.

It was Saturday afternoon and Mrs Cobbler, Bobby and Mrs Rhubarb were browsing in **Gizmo World**, the new electrical shop that had recently opened at the bottom of Pip Street. The sun was out and Bobby felt relaxed. He could forget about the blackouts (there had been four this week) while the daylight beamed around him and lights shone brightly.

"I have no idea what's going on," said Mrs Cobbler in reply. "The blackouts are a mystery that is making us all nervous. A*nd* it's stopping us enjoying the exciting new electrical gadgets we have bought in here."

There was something for everyone in **Gizmo World**, which was why the people of Pip Street had fallen in love with the shop. On this occasion, Mrs Cobbler had bought a Pride of Scotland Porridge Processor, while Mrs Rhubarb had chosen a Stanza Bonanza Automatic Poetry Maker (guaranteed to produce at least thirty-four lines per hour!).

PRIDE OF SCOTLAND PORRIDGE PROCESSOR

With their shopping done, the three of them walked home. The light was beginning to fade. Night was slowly approaching and a huge orange sun hung low in the winter sky, like a gigantic, sad egg yolk. Bobby began to feel anxious. He had butterflies and perhaps even a couple of moths in his tummy. Would there be another blackout tonight?

Outside her house, Bobby's best friend Imelda Small was playing basketball with her brother Nathan. He was wearing his brown dressing gown, because that's what he liked to do. Little Dave Pasty was keeping score. He was not wearing a dressing gown. Of any colour. No, he had on a blue duffel coat and blue jeans – Dave liked to be colour coordinated whenever possible.

Bobby went to join his friends.

"Cheer up, Bobby," said Imelda, noticing his worried face. "Are you dreading another blackout?"

Bobby nodded.

"I don't think I'll ever get used to the dark," he said. "It scares me so much my brain seems to freeze."

"You're not the only one who hates the dark, Bobby," said Nathan. "The blackouts are making everyone stressed and weird. Have you noticed?"

"I *know*," said Imelda. "I saw Mrs Rhubarb wandering about in sunglasses the other day, saying she was trying to develop her night vision, or something dingbattish, and Mr Keiths is buying up salty crisps and cans of hot dogs from the Co-op like it's the end of the world!"

At that moment, Mr Keiths sped on to the street on his speedy mobility scooter, Pegasus, tyres a-screeching.

"Get inside, kids," he called over his shoulder as he rocketed past. "Darkness is coming."

That was enough to send Bobby bombing into his house, desperate to find his torch.

14

The children followed, slamming the door behind them. Seconds later, Bobby's dad rushed in, back from the crumpet factory where he worked.

"Put out some extra chairs," he said. "I've called a meeting of street residents. Let's see if we can solve this power problem once and for all."

3
A Gathering, Gizmo World and Guilt

Mr Cobbler probably should have planned a daytime meeting, because as soon as the Rhubarbs and the Pasties arrived, the lights went out. Typical! The blackness triggered all the usual fumblings and falling-overs. Mrs Rhubarb hung her coat on Imelda; Mr Cobbler got tangled up in Nathan's dressing gown and Mr Pasty tripped over Conkers. Bobby, meanwhile, just stood very still. Like a statue playing musical statues (when the music is off).

A sudden revving cut through the chaos. It was Richard Keiths on Pegasus, but instead of parking by the kerb, he drove his mobility scooter on to the Cobblers' front garden, smashing through plant pots and squashing shrubs, like Pegasus was some kind of souped-up all-terrain quad bike for pensioners.

It did the trick, though. The powerful headlight blazed through the front windows like a beacon of hope. Bobby relaxed a little and began to breathe more calmly. The light soothed his frightened brain like oil on a rusty bike chain.

He could begin to think again.

Everyone sat down in the living room, and then Mr Cobbler spoke:

"I have talked to Bernard Sparks, Head of Power Problems at the electricity company, and he is no closer to working out what's causing the power cuts," he explained. "Pip Street is the only road affected in the neighbourhood. It's very confusing."

"Could it be robot mice made by spies?" offered Mrs Rhubarb. "Nibbling the wires?"

"Or maybe it's the local council, trying to drive us out so they can redevelop the street as an airport," said Mr Rhubarb.

"No, I think it was that bloke off the telly. The one who goes on about compost. . ." said Mr Pasty.

"It's no one from this country. This has the feel

of international meddling." said Bobby's dad, sounding like he knew what he was talking about. He didn't.

"Could be aliens," said little Dave Pasty.

"Yes, aliens," said Bobby's mum, "taking our power for a giant mother ship that's parked behind the moon." Bobby couldn't believe what he was hearing. The darkness scared him, but it seemed

20

to be sending everyone else bananas. Had they gone to pieces over the power cuts? Gone doolally over the darkness and bonkers over the blackouts? Was Bobby the only person in the room who realized this was nonsense?

No! Luckily, Imelda saw that the Pip Street people were losing the plot.

"They're talking complete blabberish!" she whispered.

But the blabberish kept coming.

"Could be the rabid pug," said one voice in the shadows. "On the loose from Rabid Pug Wood."

"Could be candle makers, trying to boost sales of candles. . ."

"Could be kittens. . ."

"Could be termites. . ."

"Could be the French. . ."

"Could be. . ."

Suddenly a terrible screeching sound cut through the crazy "could be"s. Mr Keiths was dragging his fingernails down the living-room wall (which was almost as bad as nails down a blackboard, but not quite). Everyone turned towards the sound and stared at his gnarly old face.

When the room was silent, Mr Keiths spoke.

"Gizmo World," he said, narrowing his eyes.

Everyone gasped.

"Done some thinking," he said. "We've all been taken with that new store Gizmo World, ain't we? Love the fancy gadgets and such they have in there. I seen you all coming home with your bags bursting with electrical whatnots."

Everyone nodded, thinking about the amazing devices they had bought since **Gizmo World** had opened.

"Reckon they're too strong. They're busting the system; overloading it," said Mr Keiths. "This ain't no rogue rodent or dribbling pug – it's our *greeeeeed* that's done it."

There was silence. Everyone looked a bit guilty.

Suddenly, Mr Rhubarb blustered to life. He wasn't having this! In his best actor voice – for he was an actor, after all – he said: "It's not our fault. I blame Brian Pylon, who owns the shop. He's sold us gadgets our homes cannot support. I demand he fix the problem."

There were cries of "yes, yes" and "Pylon must pay" and "I blame Brian" and "Brian who? Oh, him, right, OK".

Everyone leapt to their feet, excited and ready for action.

And so did Bobby – but only because Imelda had whispered "Do something!" and then nudged him hard in the ribs.

Imelda's tiny pointy elbow knocked the last of Bobby's blackout nerves clean out of him. He bounced into action.

"Wait!" shouted Bobby.

The people looked round.

"Don't bother Mr Pylon," said Bobby. "There is a simple way to put Mr Keiths' theory to the test."

For clever young Bobby had had an idea – a sudden, last-minute flash of inspiration. He unveiled his plan, which he quickly code-named Operation Gizmos Are Go.

All the Pip Street residents were to turn on their **Gizmo World** gadgets at exactly noon tomorrow, alongside all the usual TVs and washing machines and lights. That way, they would discover if **Gizmo World** was guilty.

If the power failed, the finger of blame could rightly point at this new store and its fancy-pants electrical products. Tomorrow, the truth would be revealed!

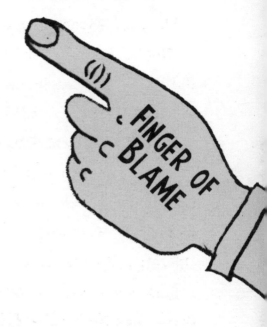

4

Operation Gizmos Are Go

The next day, the people of Pip Street plugged in their gadgets and waited for noon. News of Operation Gizmos Are Go had reached Brian Pylon, owner of **Gizmo World** and he had nervously hidden himself behind the Smalls' privet hedge to watch. A woodlouse called Gareth, perched on his shoulder, was his only companion.

28

Finally, the clock of King Ken, which chimes out across the town with its big friendly **BONGS**, chimed out across the town with a big friendly **BONG**.

BONG! On went Mrs Rhubarb's Stanza Bonanza Automatic Poetry Maker.

BONG! On went Mrs Cobbler's Pride of Scotland Porridge Processor.

BONG! On went Nathan's Bobble-Be-Gone Dressing Gown Fluff-Away Device.

BONG! On went Paddy Pasty's Pasty-Mate Potato Chopper-Upper.

BONG! On went ten TVs, six computers, seven toasters, eight kettles, five radios, eighty-seven lights and Richard Keiths' electric blanket until, by the time all twelve bongs had bonged, Pip Street was buzzing with electrical activity. You could hear the hum of the gadgets from neighbouring Dip Street and Chip Street.

Everyone came out on to the street, listening and looking. Hiding behind the hedge, Brian Pylon prayed silently to the God of Independent Electrical Retailers. (Gareth the woodlouse did nothing – fat lot of help he was.)

Would the power fail? Would the Stanza Bonanza be silenced and the Bobble-Be-Gone be bust?

No! That's the simple answer. One word. No!

The power stayed on in Pip Street.

"The power cuts can't be the fault of Gizmo World then," said Bobby.

"*YES*," whispered Brian Pylon, high-fiving Gareth before tiptoeing back to the store.

At first, everybody was relieved, but relief soon turned to anger. What *was* causing the blackouts? Questions filled the air, like a giant cloud of enquiry. But Bobby wasn't listening. He was looking. Someone was missing. Where was Jeff the Chalk? Jeff, who lived at number 1? He was a bit shy, but he usually took part in any Pip Street shilly-shallyings. But he had not been at the meeting last night, and he wasn't here now. Where could he be?

Bobby glanced over at Jeff's house. The curtains in the front window twitched. Was Jeff looking out? They twitched again and that's when

Bobby saw it. A snout! A pig's snout, nudging the window! At least, that's what it looked like. Really? Bobby couldn't believe it. He rubbed his eyes for a second, then stared again, but it was gone.

5
Training Day

The vision of the pig snout at the window bothered Bobby. Was there a pig living in Jeff's house? Surely not. Jeff was hygiene crazy. How could he allow a pig to share his home? But if it wasn't a pig at the window, what was it? Bobby felt confused. He began to doubt what he had seen. Worse, he began to doubt himself. Maybe he'd imagined it. Maybe he was unravelling,

33

like a jumper snagged on a barbed wire fence? Maybe the blackouts were turning him bonkers, just like everyone else on the street?

Bobby fretted about this all afternoon, until Imelda popped round.

"Hey, Bobster!" she shouted, bounding into his bedroom. "What's up?"

Bobby explained.

"Crackling crayfish, Bobby! This fear of the dark has gone too far," said Imelda. "It's frazzling your brain and stopping you from coming up with clever plans. And we need a plan more than ever, now. We know **Gizmo World** isn't to blame for the blackouts, so what is?"

"Don't ask me," said Bobby, nervously fiddling with the torch he kept on a string around his neck. The afternoon was dribbling away, the daylight was fading and the butterflies and moths were waking up in Bobby's tum.

"You need to stop being all scared and squealish about the dark and start thinking straight! Now!" said Imelda. "We need your brilliant Bobby brainbox in full working order or we'll never stop these blackouts. So come on, let's get you fixed up and fearless again."

Imelda's plan involved training Bobby – getting him used to the dark so that he could slowly overcome his fear of it. And that meant standing in his wardrobe. Without his torch. And Imelda shutting the doors. Just for fifteen seconds to start with, then a few more and a few more, until finally Bobby could handle sixty seconds in the pitch-black cupboard.

"A whole minute!" shouted Imelda, as Bobby tumbled out of the wardrobe with a pair of trousers on his head and lay gasping on the bedroom floor. "You can do this. You can beat your fear."

Next, Imelda covered Bobby's eyes and tiptoed around the room, occasionally poking him with a coat hanger. It was nerve-wracking for Bobby.

He nearly jumped out of his skin when Imelda first poked him, but after several minutes of practice and lots of breaks, it almost felt like fun. It certainly took Bobby's mind off the approaching night.

"Now you're getting somewhere," said Imelda. "Remember, darkness is only darkness, Bob. It doesn't really change anything. You still have Conkers and me and all your bits and bobbins around you."

And with that, Imelda jumped on Bobby and squickled him (which is when you squash someone and tickle them at the same time – a favourite pastime of these two!) The squickling perked Bobby up even more. Then he and Imelda held torches under their chins, to make spooky shadows across their faces. Then they shone them at Conkers' face, and watched his normal eyes turn into LASER EYES in the beam.

"Wow, I'm actually having fun even though we don't have the lights on and it's nearly dark outside," said Bobby.

"Exactly," said Imelda. "A blackout on the street doesn't need to be a blackout in your brain. Remember that, my old chumster. Remember that."

6
Swine Sightings

Enjoying his newfound confidence, Bobby decided to call on Jeff the Chalk that evening. It was dark outside, but the power was on and the streetlights blazed. Bobby felt all right.

Being a shy guy, Jeff didn't open the door, so Bobby shouted through the letter box. He asked if he could join Jeff on one of his chalking missions. These involved Jeff walking around the neighbourhood writing chalked messages around dog plops, encouraging owners to clean up after their pets. In response, Jeff posted a chalked message through the letter box:

NOT THIS EVENING, BOBBY. BUSY IN MY GARAGE.

"Maybe next week, then?" Bobby shouted through the letter box.

Seconds later, another chalky note appeared.

MAYBE. THINKING OF THROWING AWAY MY CHALKS, ACTUALLY. I HAVE NEW PLANS FOR STREET HYGIENE. BIG PLANS.

Bobby felt puzzled. Jeff the Chalk was, after all, a man of chalk. He wasn't Jeff the Pencil or Jeff the Email. Throwing away his chalks would be like throwing away a part of himself. Why would he do that?

"I'm surprised, Jeff," shouted Bobby. "I thought chalking round poos was what you do."

WAS WHAT I DID, came the reply. BUT THE DAWN OF A NEW ERA IS DAWNING. THAT'S ALL I CAN SAY NOW.

It made no sense to Bobby. He peeped through the letter box and saw Jeff walking off down the hall. Confused and bemused, Bobby wandered home.

7
Darkness and the Disco Cat

The following evening, Bobby sat down to watch his new favourite show: *John & Bibs Do Stuff*. Each week, John and Bibs tried out a new sport or hobby. This week it was potholing. Bobby watched John and Bibs as they squeezed through a dark, narrow opening into an underground cave. He gulped.

43

They're obviously not scared of the dark, so I shouldn't be either, he thought, when – *PFUTT* – the TV cut off and the lights went out.

A feeling of panic raced through Bobby. He fumbled for the torch on a string he wore around his neck. Not there! Where was it? Gah! Of course – up in his room where he'd left it. He tried to remember Imelda's darkness exercises; tried to tap into some of the confidence they had given him as he groped his way off the sofa and on to the floor. He remembered there was a spare torch by the TV, and crawled in its direction.

Bobby reached in front of him as he shuffled forward. Suddenly, his fingers touched something soft.

44

"Splatters!" he yelped.

"Weeooowww," said the soft something.

It was Conkers. The two grappled and wriggled on the floor, Bobby trying to restrain his springy cat, Conkers trying to escape. Conkers had the advantage, though – he could see in the dark. *Such a useful skill in a power cut.*

Conkers sprang free. Bobby hunted for the spare torch. He found it, clicked it on and darted the beam around nervously.

Two yellow eyes and a mass of sparkles glinted out from a corner. It was Conkers. Conkers with a difference, though.

45

Boy and feline had been wrestling in some art materials Bobby had left on the floor. Conkers had rolled in glue, sat on glitter and dashed across sequins – and had the fur to prove it. He looked like he was going to a disco.

Bobby tried to pull a sequin off, but Conkers hissed at him. It was rude, yes, but Bobby understood. These were trying times. Everyone was suffering.

Down the road, for example, Richard Keiths was spending hours huddled over his wind-up radio,

listening for blackout news reports and eating hot dogs which he heated on a camping stove – even when the power was on! Most people now wore high-visibility jackets, while Imelda had taken to dressing up as a fireman, complete with helmet topped off with a spotlight.

It was this spotlight that shone through Bobby's letter box now.

"Are you all right, Bobby?" called Imelda. "Have you got the power-cut colly-wobbles?"

Bobby opened the door. Imelda's light shone on Bobby, who had sprinkles of glitter stuck to his jumper, then picked out Conkers, all sequinned and silly.

"Jiggling jelly babies! What happened to you

two?" she asked, trying not to laugh.

"Victims of the power cuts," sighed Bobby.

Just then, Bobby's dad appeared at the top of the stairs. He shone his torch down on Bobby.

"We are not victims, son," he said, looking serious. "We will not let these blackouts defeat us. So pack your sports things – I have a plan. We're going to the leisure centre."

8
To the Leisure Centre

Mr Cobbler's plan was this: if we can't solve the
power cuts, let's at least avoid them.

He had called the neighbours, explaining how
the leisure centre would be light
and warm and friendly. Perhaps a
swim and a hot chocolate under
bright electrical bulbs would
revive everyone?

49

So the Cobblers, Imelda and Nathan, the Pasties and Mr and Mrs Rhubarb all trooped off by torchlight. Richard Keiths stayed hunched over his radio, listening for important blackout bulletins (there weren't any).

Everyone felt quite jolly (although Bobby gripped his torch firmly and held Imelda's hand too). Mr Cobbler's plan seemed to be working, but once inside Leisure Me Up, things changed. The people of Pip Street could avoid the dark, but they could not forget it. So instead of a swim and a hot chocolate, they signed up for courses – and not just Zumba, either.

Bobby's mum chose self-defence.

"So I can protect myself from an attack in the dark," she said.

"Splendid idea," said Mrs Rhubarb, signing up for karate. "If I can deliver a killer karate chop, I'll be safe, too. Won't I?"

Bobby's dad and Mr Pasty, never known for their love of exercise, headed for the gym and began to lift weights.

"When the power fails, you have to be strong," puffed Mr Pasty.

"Amen to that, bro," said Mr Cobbler, between grunts.

Little Dave Pasty helped by heaving more and more weights on to the dumbbells. Soon, Mr Cobbler's face was bright red, while Mr Pasty had sweated a map of Australia on to his chest.

Bobby was impressed. It even had Tasmania on it. Imelda and Nathan, meanwhile, took up archery. Nathan's dressing gown got tangled in the arrows and the bow was nearly as big as Imelda, but they kept going. They fired arrow after arrow at the bull's eye, getting closer and closer each time.

And Bobby, what did he do? Well, his fear of the dark had left him fatigued and frazzled, so he chose Jazz Yoga – or Joga. Which is calming yoga to soothing jazz music. Mmmmmm. . . Just the job for frayed nerves.

After two hours of activity, everyone walked home, tired. They turned the corner on to Pip Street – and sighed.

It was a happy sigh. A sigh from people who return to find their street illuminated. The power was back on.

Bobby could now see the mess Conkers was in. All the sequins made him look like a disco ball.

"Never mind," he said, surveying his cat. "I'll take you to Dr Mike's tomorrow."

Dr Mike was a Vet Pet Detective. *Maybe*, thought Bobby hopefully, *his detective skills extended to power cuts as well as pets*.

53

9
A Vet Visit

At the vet's the next afternoon, Dr Mike spent thirty minutes easing the stuck sequins off Conkers. While he worked, Bobby told him about the power cuts, how Conkers had got in this mess, and how everyone was nervously taking up sports they thought might help them in the dark.

"It's a mess all right, but I can't help you," said

54

Dr Mike. "No idea why the power is failing. Pets are my speciality, when it comes to detection."

Then Dr Mike asked Bobby about Jeff, who worked at the vet's.

"Have you seen him around?" he said. "He lives near you, right?"

"Yes, over the road," said Bobby, "but I've hardly seen him lately. He stays in his house."

"We had a PPI here recently," Dr Mike continued.

"A PPI?" said Bobby.

"Sorry – pet detective lingo," said Dr Mike. "PPI means Pygmy Pig Incident. Not long ago, I found a small pig on the doorstep, dumped there in a box. It looked sick so I took it in. Jeff was seeing to it, but when I checked on them later, the pig was staring at Jeff. And I mean *staring*."

Dr Mike pulled off a particularly sticky sequin. Conkers hissed.

"When I talked to Jeff, he seemed blank," Dr Mike continued. "He hasn't been at work since and the pig's disappeared, too. That's what I call strange. I'll check it out soon, but I have been busy hunting down a tortoise who stole a lettuce from a greengrocer. He was last seen heading for the cover of a rockery in somebody's front garden."

Bobby's brain fizzed when he heard about the PPI. Perhaps he really had seen a snout at the window of Jeff's house? Perhaps there was a pig living there? And not just any pig – the pygmy pig that had stared at Jeff? Bobby chewed this over, like a gobstopper of mystery, as he walked home with Conkers in the late-afternoon gloom. Back on Pip Street, he glanced at Jeff's place.

"Crumbling cliff faces!" gasped Bobby.

A glistening snout sniffed at the window and two beady eyes stared out.

57

"Ha! A pig! Yes! I'm not going mad after all," said Bobby.

Bobby stared at the pig. It was small, black and bristly with tiny dark eyes. The pig stared back. This went on for two, maybe three seconds, until Imelda skipped up the road, dressed as a spy.

"Did you see that?" exclaimed Bobby, pulling his eyes away and shaking his head. That piggy stare had made him feel a little strange.

"Shhh," said Imelda, pulling the big collar of her coat up around her tiny face.

"I'm under cover."

Which gave Bobby an idea.

58

10
Peeping, Prying, Looking and Spying

Spying! That was Bobby's idea. Spying on Jeff.

Now, spying isn't really OK in normal life. It's a bit nosy, isn't it? And nobody likes a noser. But this wasn't normal life, this was "special times", when blackouts blitzed the houses and darkness lurked all around like a champion expert lurker. . .

"I need to see into Jeff's garage," said Bobby to

Imelda. "I think he's up to something in there and I'm pretty sure he has a pig inside, too."

"A pig? Why?" asked Imelda.

"No idea," said Bobby. "That's what I'm trying to work out, but I need a little help from a little friend."

"That's me!" said Imelda, looking excited.

"Exactly! Keep watch," said Bobby. "And if you  see Jeff, sound the alarm by doing that duck impression you do. Then run for it!"

So, with Conkers swinging in his basket, Bobby and Imelda flattened themselves against trees, tiptoed behind parked cars and ran across the road to Jeff's garage.

"It's beginning to get dark and the power could go off at any time, Bobby," said Imelda, as she took up her position behind a wheelie bin. "Be quick."

Bobby noticed windows along the side of Jeff the Chalk's garage, but they were high up. How could he peep in? He looked around for something to stand on, until Conkers, scratching at the basket like a cat who really wants out, ruined Bobby's concentration. Hurriedly, Bobby opened the basket and Conkers sprang out, but instead of running home, Conkers darted down a narrow path into Jeff's garden.

"Oh cheese puffs," muttered Bobby, as Conkers disappeared. Now he would have to find him.

Nervously, Bobby tiptoed after Conkers. He

followed the path, turned into the garden and. . .

"Triple fudge sundaes," he said.

What a sight! A terrifying animal stand-off was taking place. Conkers's black fur was puffed out and his tail looked like a gigantic loo brush. Opposite, standing and staring with eyes as dark as night, was the pig.

The pig was small; its eyes were small, too. Little mean eyes, like dark pools of piggy naughtiness.

The pig fixed Conkers with those eyes for a few more seconds, then it raced up the path and nudged open a low wooden door in the wall with its snout. Conkers followed and, without thinking, Bobby chased after both animals and squeezed in through the opening. He stood up to find himself inside Jeff's garage. Slowly, his eyes grew accustomed to the dim light and as he looked around, the hairs on the back of his neck rose.

There was a penny-farthing propped against one wall, but that wasn't what grabbed Bobby's attention. No, Bobby was gazing at the vast machine in front of him. Huge wheels, thick tyres, a cab full of controls, a steering wheel wider than a family-sized pie and, at the front, two enormous

63

nozzles. Bobby marvelled at this machine. It was impressive, but scary, too.

"It's some kind of truck with trunks," Bobby muttered.

Then his eyes picked out the writing on the bonnet: Jeffatronic 5000.

For yes, it was the Jeffatronic 5000 and it had been made by – you've guessed it – Jeff. Nobody knew that before becoming a vet nurse, Jeff had worked for a few months at NASA, the American space agency. He had learned fast, becoming a skilled mechanic with a flair for astrophysics, and now he had used these skills to build a mighty vehicle.

As Bobby gazed at the Jeffatronic, wondering what it could be used for, the pig came racing past, followed by Conkers. Conkers was moving in a funny way – a bit jerkily, like a robot cat might move – but before Bobby could get to him, Jeff came in through a door from the house. Quickly, Bobby hid behind some tyres. Jeff flicked on a light, admired his machine for a few moments, then grabbed a huge cable with a giant plug at one end and pushed it into a socket in the side of the cab.

At that moment, the garage lights flickered once, twice, three times – then went out. Pip Street was having another blackout.

11
Crumpets and Considerations

Bobby remained hidden behind the tyres. He felt a little scared of the darkness, but not utterly paralysed by it. Good. Imelda's exercises had helped, Bobby realized, and probably the Joga too. Instead of panicking and going blank, he kept calm and focused. A little while later, Jeff pulled the plug out of his machine and the lights in the garage pinged back on again.

"Fully charged at last," Jeff said. He was talking to the pig, which was standing beside him. "So tonight, we start."

Then Jeff walked back into the house, with the pig skipping along beside. Conkers went to follow them, still doing his weird, jerky robot walk that was nothing like the tigerish grace Conkers usually displayed, but the pig stared at Conkers again, stopping him in his tracks, before disappearing inside.

At last, Bobby could move. He picked up Conkers and raced outside, bumping into Imelda, who was patrolling the street.

"I need to talk to you about what I've seen," said Bobby. "And Nathan too. Go get him and then meet me in my kitchen – sharpish!"

Bobby's kitchen was empty. His parents had obviously fled to Leisure Me Up with all the other neighbours as soon as the blackout had struck. But as it had only been short, the power was now back on. Power on meant toaster working. Toaster working meant Bobby could make King Crumpets* – one after the other, after the other – for him and his two friends to feast on.

King Crumpets are toffee filled crumpets – and super delicious. They were invented by Bobby and Imelda, which you would know if you had read A Crumpety Calamity – and if you haven't read it, read it pronto (but finish this one first, or things are going to get confusing).

As they ate, Bobby told Imelda and Nathan what he had seen in Jeff's garage.

"It can't just be a coincidence that the power failed right after Jeff plugged in his machine," said Bobby. "Because it came back on after he unplugged it. Which means the power cuts are connected to the Jeffatronic 5000."

"Its engine must have to be charged with so much electricity that it takes up all the power that would normally go into our homes," said Nathan. "We have to persuade Jeff to stop using it – but how? We don't even know what it is!"

"Jeff said something about 'tonight we start' in his garage," added Bobby, "so I'll keep watch from my window later; see what I can see."

"Jeff spoke?" Nathan said in surprise.

"But what does the pig have to do with any of this?" asked Imelda.

"The pig? Hmmm," said Bobby, feeling his brain scrabbling for the answer.

"I just know the pig is involved somehow," said Bobby. "I'm not sure how yet – that dingy garage has left me a bit shaken – but I can sense it. Smell it, even. . ."

Well, it was a pig, after all.

12
All Hail the Jeffatronic 5000

After eating, Imelda gave Bobby a few more darkness training exercises (using the cupboard under the stairs this time) and then she and Nathan went home. Bobby looked for Conkers. Usually, when crumpets were being cooked, Conkers would hang around, hoping to lick some toffee off the plates. But not today. Instead, Bobby found Conkers in the living room, sitting on the windowsill. He was staring towards Jeff's house, hardly blinking. When Bobby called him, Conkers did not move. When Bobby offered him a plate of Fish Lumps (his favourite food), still Conkers did not move. He seemed to be in a trance.

Bobby went upstairs to watch over the street, his mind full of power cuts and pigs and poorly pussycats. It seemed that Jeff had been acting strangely since the pig had stared at him in the vet's. Now Conkers was acting strangely, too – and the pig had fixed him with its beady eyes in Jeff's garden.

It's like they have both been hypnotized, thought Bobby, a shiver of fear running up his spine, *I just don't really understand why or how or. . .*

Suddenly, a shaft of light beamed out from Jeff's garage. Jeff was dressed in blue overalls and he pushed the doors open before disappearing inside.

Then, making only the softest of kittenish purrs, the Jeffatronic 5000 emerged.

Five headlights blazed, but Bobby could still make out Jeff, sitting in the driving seat, with the pig sitting next to him. The two drove up Pip Street and round the corner. There was nothing else for it: Bobby had to follow!

13
The Chase is On!

Snatching his coat, stumbling into his trainers, Bobby rushed out of the house. His heart was pounding with excitement, but not dread. Bobby's darkness training had paid off and, with the moon out and the streetlights on, the curious Bobby – the Bobby who could not resist a mystery – was back in charge.

Bobby tracked the Jeffatronic 5000 along the quiet night-time streets. On and on it travelled.

76

On and on Bobby followed. Finally, the machine began to make a low whooshing sound. The huge nozzles descended and as Bobby watched, its purpose suddenly became obvious. It was for sucking. Sucking up mess. Sucking up – *of course!* – dog poos.

Jeff's life was dedicated to cleaner streets and plop-free pavements. Now he had developed a machine that could make his hygiene dreams a reality. This was what he'd meant by "big plans". This machine could rid a whole neighbourhood of mess in one night. It was poo cleaning on an epic scale.

As Bobby watched the Jeffatronic 5000, he noticed that it was sucking up more than just dog poos. The leaves from bushes, a traffic cone and a child's scooter were all whooshed inside. Benches strained at their foundations. Fences wobbled and leaned towards the nozzles. Tree branches bent low, touching its gaping mouth.

Bobby felt alarmed. This was too much power; too much sucky-uppyness.

This was street hygiene gone mad.

It was wrong, with a capital WR. But what could Bobby do to tackle a man on a mission, a machine, and a mean-looking pig?

14
Bobby Discovers the Truth

The next morning, when Bobby woke up, Conkers was sitting on his bed. Bobby reached out to tickle him, just as he had done a thousand times before, but this time Conkers sprang away and jumped on to the bedroom floor. Next, Conkers began pacing around and around in robotic circles, stopping occasionally to stare at the corner of the room, as if a presence were sitting there, staring back. It gave Bobby the shudders.

"Stop acting so spooky," said Bobby.

As the word *spooky* fell from Bobby's lips, he remembered! His new book! Full of strange, dangerous creatures, including – *DUR DUR DURRRRR* – the SPOOKHOG!

Goosebumps spread up Bobby's arms. He rummaged for *Folklore's Freaky Creatures* under his bed and then quickly turned the pages until he found the spookhog. As he studied the picture,

81

realization crashed over him, like a giant wave of understanding.

Suddenly, Bobby saw everything. Of course! The pig living in Jeff's home wasn't a pig at all – it was a spookhog! It had hypnotized Conkers but first, it had hypnotized Jeff, frazzling him with its mischievous mind waves. It had made Jeff mad and bad, and more Jeff-like than ever, and the mad, bad, ultra Jeff had built the Jeffatronic 5000, a machine so powerful it drained all the electricity from Pip Street.

Bobby blew out a long, slow breath. He had solved the mystery now – joined the dots and filled in the blanks and got to the very bottom of it all. But what next?

Bobby read to the end of the page. The last line said:

The spookhog's victim may only be cured if the spookhog itself is cleansed of its evil powers.

That was all. Not much to go on. Bobby frowned as the truth slowly sank in: if he was going to help Jeff and Conkers and restore power to Pip Street, *first* he had to cure that pig.

15
Ugly Scenes on Pip Street

Bobby was pondering the piggy problem when Imelda popped her head round his bedroom door.

"What's up, Bobsicle?" she said.

Bobby explained everything and Imelda's eyes grew wider and wider as she took in the crazy tale.

"So the blackouts and Conkers and Jeff acting weird are all because of one small, naughty pig," said Imelda. "Wow!"

"Yes, wow," said Bobby, "but what do we do about it?"

Imelda frowned and was about to speak, when the children heard Mr Keiths speeding to a stop on the street outside. They looked out of the window and saw that Pegasus had pulled up in front of Jeff the Chalk's house. Jeff had just emerged for the first time in days and the two men were talking – at least, Mr Keiths was saying something, but Jeff seemed to look straight through him and, after a few moments, wandered off down the street.

Bobby and Imelda raced outside to find out what Jeff had said.

"I asked him where he had been these last few days," said Mr Keiths. "And what he felt about the power cuts, but he said nothing and chalked nothing. He seemed strange; different."

More street residents came to ask about Jeff – Mrs Rhubarb, Mr Pasty and Mr Cobbler joined the huddle around Pegasus.

"Why did Jeff not reply?" Mr Cobbler asked Mr Keiths. "He's often quiet, but he usually replies with a message in chalk!"

"And why isn't he bothered by the blackouts?" asked Mr Pasty, in amazement. "I mean, we're certainly bothered by the blackouts, aren't we?"

"Yes, yes we are," said Mrs Rhubarb. "How can he not care? Extraordinary!"

The blackouts had made everyone jittery and suspicious. Now, they stared at the disappearing figure of Jeff. They frowned at him. They fixed him with their furious glares. They remembered their Leisure Me Up skills, too, and suddenly Mrs Rhubarb's hands formed into karate choppers. Mr Pasty and Mr Cobbler cracked their knuckles and clenched their fists and waved them at Jeff as he walked away. Everyone felt tense, angry, and really very threatened by Jeff and his funny behaviour.

That was until the sound of jazz music floated through the air, instantly filling everyone with a mellow feeling. It was Bobby! He was running towards the group, holding a portable CD player, from which Joga music tinkled – it was extremely soothing.

Mrs Rhubarb relaxed her karate-chop hands. Mr Cobbler and Mr Pasty unclenched their fists. The assembled folk breathed out and then looked at each other with embarrassment, as though they had sleep-walked on to the street and woken to find they had no trousers on.

Shameful scenes, indeed, but this is what power cuts did to people. They turned neighbour against neighbour; guinea pig against hamster; lollipop man against lollipop woman.

"Sorry, son," said Mr Cobbler, sighing. "We're all just a bit tense, that's all, and Jeff got us worked up. The power cuts are getting to us, you see? Terrible, really. . ."

The people went silently home, but Bobby and Imelda hung around on the street, waiting for Jeff to come back. A few minutes later, Jeff appeared and the children followed him as he walked back to his house.

"I know what you're up to," Bobby said. "I've seen the Jeffatronic 5000. It's too strong, Jeff. Let it go."

Jeff stopped suddenly. He turned round and looked at Bobby with his weird blank stare, only this time, Bobby caught a glint of irritation in those dark eyes. Just for a second. Then, silently, Jeff turned and disappeared into his house.

16
What's the Plan?

Back in Bobby's room, Bobby turned to Imelda. "I never thought I would see neighbours feeling so angry towards another neighbour," he said, frowning.

"I know," said Imelda. "Ponky old power cuts! They are getting everyone jiggered up."

"That's why we have to do something," said Bobby. "Before an actual fight breaks out. We are the only two people on Pip Street who fully understand what's happening. We have to cure that pig before there's more trouble. I want Jeff and Conkers back, just as they used to be, and the lights on and everything normal again. We need a plan!"

"You're right," said Imelda. "This power cut pandemonium has gone too far and that pig definitely needs a tip-top telling off, too. But Bobby, there's hardly any time for plans! Jeff has to be stopped right now!"

Imelda had started hopping about with excitement and tension.

"We can't just ask Jeff to stop, I've tried that already," said Bobby.

"OK," said Imelda, hopping. "Can we go into Jeff's garage and break the Jeffatronic somehow?"

"No," said Bobby. "That's too mean, and besides, Jeff could probably fix it."

"True," said Imelda, this time pacing the room. "Can we steal the pig, put it on a train and send it far away?"

"Too risky," said Bobby, pacing as well. "What if it hypnotized us, too, just like it has hypnotized Jeff and Conkers? We need to somehow get rid of the evil powers inside the pig, not simply chase it away to cause more trouble in another town."

"Then what?" shrieked Imelda. "What can we do? We have no plan at all!"

"Perhaps that's the point," said Bobby, standing still suddenly. "Maybe, this time, the plan is to have no plan at all..."

17
Extraordinary Scenes of Suction

After coming up with the no-plan plan, Bobby and Imelda agreed to follow Jeff again that night. Imelda went home and Bobby spent the afternoon quietly reading. He felt oddly calm as dusk began to inch its way on to Pip Street, fading the colours of the day to a winter grey. Then, a few moments later, the lights went out again. Another blackout!

By torchlight, Bobby gathered up his sports kit and joined the people of Pip Street as they trudged off to Leisure Me Up, to escape the darkness. By the time the weary residents returned, the power was on again. Bobby went upstairs and sat at his window, waiting for Jeff to appear. It had to be soon – the power being back on meant the Jeffatronic was charged and ready.

Conkers was staring out too, waiting and watching for the spookhog.

It made Bobby sad to see Conkers so changed, but it made him more determined than ever to put things right.

As Bobby watched, he listened to his Joga soundtrack on his headphones to stay calm. Finally, Jeff's garage doors opened and the Jeffatronic's headlights beamed out. Jeff was driving and there, beside him, was the pig.

Both Jeff and the pig looked at Bobby. Four eyes stared hard at his two. Bobby ducked. When he looked up again, the Jeffatronic had turned the corner of Pip Street.

"Show time!" said Bobby, running downstairs and sprinting on to the street. Almost immediately, a tiny figure appeared at his elbow.

Bobby smiled. It was Imelda, of course, with her archer's bow and quiver of arrows over her shoulder. Bobby was pleased to have his compact comrade with him. He hoped that, when the time came, he would know how to sort out the pig and save Jeff and Conkers, but he might need a little help, too.

The two friends followed the Jeffatronic past Dip Street and Chip Street as it headed for the edge of town.

"It's going to the playing fields," said Bobby.

The playing fields were always dotted with dog plops. Jeff knew it. Bobby knew it.

Once there, the nozzles of the Jeffatronic lowered and a whooshing sound started.

"So it begins," murmured Bobby.

Bobby and Imelda watched as the Jeffatronic drove along, sucking up grass, dog poos, even a football net, each item illuminated by its vast headlights. They stood motionless, staring at this huge machine, wondering how it could be beaten, feeling small (which was not hard for Imelda, but anyway...).

Their awe soon turned to shock when the two friends were distracted by a movement. There was a dark shape edging along the hedge about thirty metres from one of the nozzles.

With a stomach flip of pure panic, Bobby realized that the dark shape was shaped like Conkers. And that it was shaped like Conkers because it *was* Conkers!

Under the spookhog's evil spell, Conkers had silently followed his piggy master. Now, he was moving dangerously close to the Jeffatronic's nozzles.

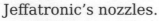

"No, Conkers," shouted Bobby. "Don't get any nearer!"

Conkers didn't stop. He marched towards the deadly machine. Bobby knew he couldn't run to him in time. Conkers was too far off.

"Stop, Conkers, stop!" yelled Bobby.

But the bewitched feline kept on walking. Bobby stared in disbelief and fear, as Conkers took more steps; steps that would put him within suction range of the machine. . .

. . .when suddenly a thin, silvery arrow shot through the moonlit sky and landed centimetres from the cat's advancing paws.

Conkers leapt in surprise and confusion and skipped away.

Imelda! She had loosed an arrow and shocked Conkers to safety. All those archery lessons had paid off.

Bobby sagged with relief, but not for long. For suddenly he felt as though a fire had been lit in his belly – and it wasn't indigestion. No, it was a fire of pure strength (with sparks of derring-do, too!). He knew what he had to do.

Bobby placed his hands on Imelda's shoulders.

"Find Conkers," he said. "Keep him safe. I have a spookhog to battle."

18
Wrestling the Demon

Bobby ran towards the Jeffatronic 5000. He was fizzing with energy now. Seeing his cat under the pig's evil spell and in danger was the final straw. Enough. Enough already! Enough by at least one hundred per cent!

Running hard, his headphones bouncing around his neck, Bobby caught up with the mighty machine and waved frantically at Jeff. Jeff glanced at Bobby and frowned, but continued driving, sucking up grass, twigs, drinks cans, moths, earthworms, vole whiskers, plastic bags, spider hotels and the occasional dog poo, too.

"Stop it, Jeff," yelled Bobby.

Jeff ignored him.

"This isn't you, Jeff," Bobby shouted. "It's the pig! The pig has hypnotized you. It's a spookhog, Jeff – you cannot trust it."

Jeff didn't seem to hear Bobby, but the spookhog did. With an ear-splitting squeal and a mighty piggy leap, it jumped from the cab and flew through the air, aiming straight for Bobby.

KERBOOSH!

Four tiny trotters punched his chest, knocking him to the ground with a thud.

Then the tussling began. Boy and spookhog wrestled on the damp earth. There were squeals from the spookhog and shouts from Bobby. Bobby could hear Imelda shrieking in alarm. He wrestled and wriggled for what seemed like hours. It was tiring. The spookhog may have been small, but it was strong. *Really* strong.

To make matters worse, Bobby and the spookhog had wrestled into the path of the Jeffatronic 5000. They were just beyond the reach of its suction power, but with every moment, the machine crept closer.

"Move, Bobby, get out of the way!" shouted Imelda from the hedge, where she held Conkers.

Then she dropped the cat and, grabbing her bow, fired arrow after arrow at the Jeffatronic. She was trying to pierce the tyres or at least distract Jeff. No luck. The arrows bounced off the thick rubber while Jeff just kept on sucking, undeterred, like a man possessed. (Of course he *was* a man possessed, so we can expect nothing less from him.)

Things were looking desperate. Bobby was being thoroughly pummelled by the spookhog and now, surely, the Jeffatronic would suck our brave hero clean up...

Or would it?

For just then, Bobby had an idea. A clever idea. An inspired idea. A last-minute, just-in-time, not-a-moment-too-soon, crumbs-that-was-close idea!

Grabbing the headphones from around his neck, he clamped them on to the spookhog's ears and cranked up the volume. The Joga music flooded out, its soothing notes pouring straight into the spookhog's brain. The possessed porcine paused. It stopped stamping on Bobby. Its muscles relaxed. Its body went limp. Its once-crazed eyes turned dreamy and mellow.

Bingo!

The Joga music had triumphed again! Its calm, gentle sound could not be resisted, even by a spookhog!

This was Bobby's chance. Grabbing the pig tightly, he jumped up. Another child would have run away. Another child would have dropped the pig and fled home. But Bobby was not another child and he had no intention of behaving like one.

Instead, he did something extraordinary. Something dangerous. Something a little bit mad. He stepped out in front of the Jeffatronic's nozzle.

"AAARRRGGGHHHH!!!"

Bobby yelled, as the suction immediately pulled him forward, nearly plucking him off his feet. His hair, clothes and even his eyelashes were dragged towards the mighty mouth.

"GRRRRR!"

Bobby roared, struggling to keep his footing, gripping the spookhog tighter.

Jeff continued to drive towards Bobby, his eyes blank. He really just did not care! The suction increased with every millimetre that he advanced. Bobby stumbled, his body lurching forward.

"Just a little more," he gasped.

"One ... more ... second..." he groaned, fighting with the last of his strength.

Finally, when he could hold on no more, Bobby shouted:

"SPOOKHOG BE GONE!"

And let the wicked creature go.

The tiny pig rocketed into the nozzle. A shrill oinking issued from deep within the machine. Sparks exploded from the engine and the Jeffatronic shook from side to side several times, before shuddering to a stop.

Silence fell. And so did Bobby. Exhausted, he collapsed to the ground.

Imelda rushed over.

"Are you all right?" she gasped, helping him to sit up.

"Yes, I'm OK," said Bobby.

Then they noticed Jeff. He had jumped down from the cab, his face warm and worried, but full of friendship – it was the true face of Jeff.

"Jeff," whispered Bobby. "You're back. It's over."

113

Jeff nodded, gulping back tears. Then Conkers came and rubbed his cheek against Bobby's hand. "Conkers! You're all better, too," said Imelda, grinning. "Amazing!"

Oh happy, happy moment! But where was the spookhog?

An oinking came from deep inside the Jeffatronic. Not the crazed, squealy oink of the spookhog, though. It was a gentle, shy oink that seemed to say, "Excuse me, sorry to bother you, but could you possibly help me out?"

Jeff, Imelda and Bobby ran to the machine and Jeff prised it open. A mucky mess of litter and doggie doings tumbled out, and then finally, tiptoeing slowly forward, came a pig.

It was the same pig, only different. The mean eyes of the spookhog had transformed into the kind, jolly little eyes of a kind, jolly little pig.

The spookhog's wiry black bristles had been completely sucked out, leaving the pig naked in its clean pink skin. It looked as soft as a baby's bottom, and less likely to get nappy rash, too.

"I think the Jeffatronic sucked the evil clean out of that hog," said Bobby. "He's cured!"

The pig trotted over and greeted the assembled watchers, nudging its snout into their legs, then nuzzling Conkers. It was a beautiful scene and Imelda, Bobby and Jeff laughed gratefully as the sun rose, bathing them in gentle warmth.

The trio walked back to Pip Street: Bobby with Conkers under his arm, Imelda with her bow slung over her shoulder, and Jeff carrying a small, pink pig with gentle, dewy eyes.

19
Power to the People

As the three friends turned on to Pip Street, Mrs Rhubarb, setting off for her morning jog, saw them and sent up a cry. They looked like soldiers returning from a war. Imelda was pale and her hair was full of leaves; Jeff was as white as milk and Bobby was bruised and covered in mud. The neighbours spilled on to the street to greet them.

"Where have you *been*?" gasped Mrs Cobbler.

"What's happened?"

"I'm not sure you would believe me if I told you," said Bobby, "but I'm certain the power will be back on tonight and every night for ever more."

"Hoorah!" yelled all the neighbours.

Of course, Bobby was right. With the evil sucked out of the spookhog, Jeff was released from its hypnotic powers and his desire to drive the Jeffatronic 5000 on epic poo-clearing missions disappeared completely. In fact, Jeff abandoned his machine up on those playing fields, and it was taken away by the council and used for scrap.

Now, with the Jeffatronic no longer using all the power, Pip Street's electricity supply was safe again.

Huzzah and bally-hoo!

What better way to celebrate the electricity being on for good than a trip to **Gizmo World**?!

So after breakfast (cooked, of course – this was not a day for muesli), everyone headed to the store, chatting excitedly. Owner Brian Pylon welcomed them warmly.

Bobby's parents bought him new headphones to replace the ones that had got sucked into the Jeffatronic 5000. They  also bought him a Sock It To Me – for locating lost socks. (*Lost a sock? The Sock It To Me will sniff out your missing footwear in moments...*)

Eager to keep his hair neat and tidy, Mr Cobbler bought a Chipper Chopper – For Happy Haircuts At Home. Imelda, meanwhile, chose a Perky Twizzler, for creating super-curly hair.

"But you already have curly hair," said Bobby.

"Don't care," said Imelda.

As for Jeff the Chalk, he bought a flashing collar for his pig, which he had named Sausage.

SO SAUSAGE CAN COME WITH ME ON NIGHT-TIME CHALKING MISSIONS, Jeff chalked in his notepad, by way of explanation.

That evening, Bobby, Imelda and Jeff sat watching *John & Bibs Do Stuff* together. This time, John and Bibs were trying country dancing. Jolly!

Conkers was asleep on Bobby's lap and Sausage was snoozing next to Jeff.

"I'm so pleased everything turned out all right," said Bobby. "It's good to have you back, Jeff."

IT'S GOOD TO BE BACK, BOBBY, chalked Jeff on a notepad. FOR EVER MORE, I SHALL BE JEFF THE CHALK. YOU HAVE SAVED ME AND LEARNED A GREAT LESSON ABOUT YOURSELF, TOO.

"Really?" said Bobby.

"Yes, of course," piped up Imelda. "Jeff is right. You have cured the spookhog and beaten the darkness. And you were scared of the dark, right?

So you win!"

That night, Bobby slept with Conkers on his chest and his night light off. He had nothing to fear from the dark now. He slept a peaceful sleep, dreaming of nothing in particular, snuggled under his duvet on a Pip Street that had, thanks to his braveness and brilliance, returned to normal.

This is probably a good time to end this story, isn't it? Let us leave Bobby and Conkers for now; leave them to their peaceful slumbers. Shh, quietly, come away. Let them have their rest. They deserve it, after all, don't you think?

TURN OVER
FOR MORE

FUN

QUIZ TIME!

SO YOU'VE GOT TO THE END
OF THE BOOK. WELL DONE YOU.
BUT HAVE YOU BEEN PAYING
ATTENTION? REALLY? THERE'S
ONLY ONE WAY TO FIND OUT.
WITH A QUIZ! FIVE QUESTIONS,
STARTING NOW...

QUESTION 1

Does Jeff the Chalk

A) Send text messages B) Write chalk messages
C) Send smoke signals

QUESTION 2

What is Bobby scared of?
A) The dark B) Spiders C) Belly button fluff

QUESTION 3

Imelda Small has
A) Straight hair B) Grey hair C) Curly hair

QUESTION 4

Who lives in Rabid Pug Wood?
A) The Spookhog B) The Rabid Pug C) Conkers

QUESTION 5

Where could Conkers go covered in sequins?
A) A disco B) A barn dance C) Gizmo World

A PIGGY PICKLE WORDSEARCH

```
M  A  B  K  E  J  A  S  U  S
A  K  R  I  M  E  L  D  A  G
R  A  T  C  Z  F  J  O  V  A
D  R  A  B  H  F  J  E  F  F
H  C  Y  J  B  A  I  N  K  T
C  G  B  O  K  T  L  H  N  O
O  D  B  G  R  R  L  K  P  R
N  S  O  A  Y  O  D  T  I  C
K  P  B  B  G  N  E  A  P  H
E  R  F  F  P  I  G  G  Y  K
R  H  J  U  P  C  I  E  P  E
S  P  O  O  K  H  O  G  R  S
```

HAVE A LOOK FOR THESE HIDDEN WORDS:

Spookhog   Imelda   Pip
Jeff   Joga   Jeffatronic
Chalk   Dark   Piggy
Bobby   Conkers   Torch

DO YOU KNOW WHICH ANIMALS THESE PRINTS BELONG TO?

A   B   C   D

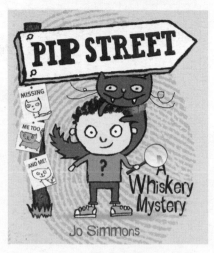

Have you seen Bobby Cobbler's cat, Conkers?
He looks like a miniature black panther (on a good day).

But Conkers is nowhere to be found.
He's not on Pip Street!

He's disappeared — along with lots of other cats.
What in the name of frying pans is going on?

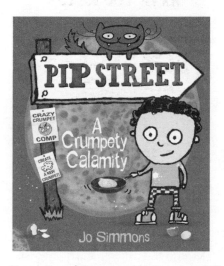

Ahoy there! Do you like crumpets?
Well, not many people on Pip Street do,
which is why Bobby Cobbler's dad, head of
the local crumpet factory, is throwing a taste-tastic
crumpet competition — to make them more
scrumptious and exciting!

Who will win? Who will come last? And who borrowed
my blue pen? (I'd like it back, please.)

Jo Simmons lives in Brighton with her husband and two children. They share their home with a dog called Betty and a cat called Pickle (before you ask – no, they don't get on. Pickle lives upstairs; Betty lives downstairs).

Jo likes sleeping, running and eating ice cream straight from the pot, though not all at the same time, of course. That would be silly. And impossible.

www.visitpipstreet.com